FRANZEL'S REVENGE!

TALES OF THE STEEL QUARTERS

KYRI DEMBY

CONTENTS

CHAPTER ONE
The Beginning

Mr. Bashara glanced around the principal's sparse looking office where he was seated with his wife just across from the principal herself, who was currently on a phone call. The walls were packed with pictures of awards that exceptional students had won on behalf of the school. Looking at the smiling faces in those pictures made his chest tighten a bit.

Mr. Bashara was used to receiving calls from the school with reports of either one of his twin daughters' bad behaviors, but he has never been called to a physical meeting. It was never really necessary. But this time, the principal demanded to see both parents because the twins had caused some big trouble this time.

Seated in Principal Blue's office for quite a long time with her beating around the bush, and not explaining the exact offense the twins had committed, Mr. Bashara was feeling quite uneasy.

"I'm sorry, Mr. and Mrs. Bashara, but that call was important," the principal apologized as she adjusted her glasses and leaned forward on her desk, "I understand that you are busy people, so I'll be quick with the rest."

"Which of them is it this time?" Mr. Bashara interjected in a tired tone, folding his beefy arms across his broad chest. It was still morning but his sleeves were already rolled up and his brown eyes looked weary.

"Well sir, it is huh–it's the both of them. Liya was caught bullying a fellow classmate, and Mira insulted her science teacher," the principal replied cautiously, tapping her perfectly manicured fingers softly against her desk.

She was trying to be careful as the Basharas were influential people and one of the school's leading sponsors and she didn't want to jeopardize losing their support.

"Wow," Mrs. Bashara finally spoke up as she buried her face in her palms. She was so frustrated and embarrassed. Frustrated at the fact that her daughters were always on the edge of one trouble or the other.

"They both will have detention as usual because there was no serious physical damage done. But that's exactly why I asked to see you both," Principal Blue said, clearing her throat.

"Yes?" Mr. Bashara probed, looking up at the principal's face.

"This time, your daughter's actions came so close to getting them suspended from school. And as much as I'd really hate to do that, I'll be left with no choice if anything of this sort should happen again. And by the way, the other parents are starting to get worried too," she explained sincerely.

"We understand, ma'am" and "Thank you," Mrs. Bashara replied when she realized that her husband had no intention of responding calmly.

"Thank you for your time," the principal said with a smile as she rose to her feet to signify the end of the meeting.

"Thank you, Principal Blue," Mr. Bashara finally said, standing to his feet, "we'll work harder at keeping our girls in check."

The principal nodded in response and breathed a sigh of relief as the Basharas walked out of her office. The school was doing its best to correct the mischievous girls, and now it was left for their parents to figure out ways to get the girls to listen to instruction.

** ** ** ** ** **

Mira Bashara and her identical twin sister Liya, walked into their exquisite white house-the most beautiful one on the block, in fact-giggling and bouncing their curly, long black hair, as they hummed to a song they heard in school earlier that day. They walked past their mother, who was making a batter on the kitchen table and headed straight for the stairs.

"You're late for prayers young ladies, and at least say hi to your mother," their father said, walking down the stairs.

"Who cares about some silly prayer?" Liya mumbled under her breath as she rolled her eyes knowing her mother heard what she said.

"Aliyah!" Her mom exclaimed, looking shocked. Mrs. Bashara always took their five prayers of the day very seriously and she sank into despondency knowing that her daughters didn't.

"It's Liya, mom. Just Liya," she replied sharply.

"You can't talk to your mom like that, Aliyah," her father scolded, as he made his way to the end of the stairs where they stood.

"Right. Here we go again," Mira said under her breath, rolling her large brown eyes.

"What did you say, Amirah?" her father asked in a strict voice.

"Nothing," she retorted.

"Good because I will not have you being rude to your mother or me, while you're living under our roof. Do you understand me? Now, go to your rooms," he ordered, trying his best to not raise his voice.

By the heavens, he loved his daughters but he just couldn't understand why they were so difficult. Their mother often said it was because they are girls, but was it? His friends had female children too, and they never complained about such rude behavior.

"By the way, after you put your things away in your rooms, I want you both to come back to the living room, we need to talk," Mr. Bashara called out, suddenly remembering his meeting with the principal that morning.

The girls paused grudgingly on the stairs, wondering what was on their fathers mind this time but didn't take heed to his command. Much later, about an hour, they came back down from their rooms–but only because they were hungry.

After they finished eating, they were about to make their way back to their rooms when their father stopped them.

"Sit down, ladies," he said in a voice they could not disobey and they both returned to their seats at the table, "Your mother and I met with your principal today."

The girls shifted uneasily in their chairs as they remembered that their science teacher asked to meet with their parents just a while back but they refused to relay the information to them.

"Your principal told us about all of the trouble you both have been causing lately. I have to say that I am very disappointed," Mr. Bashara said calmly, " What exactly is wrong with the both of you? I'd really like to know. What do you want? Bullying a fellow student? Insulting a teacher? Why, ladies? What is wrong with you?"

"Look, dad. Can we not do this?" Liya spoke first. She was the most sharp witted of the both of them. Mira on the other hand was a product of her sister's influence.

"Do what?" her father asked, looking confused.

"This thing where you act solemn and pretend like you care. Because you don't.

You guys don't even understand us-you or mum," she retorted.

"What?" her father asked, staring at his daughter's face to be sure she was alright.

"Yes. I said that. You and mom were never even around while we were growing up, remember? You were abroad and mom was only home for a few days a week. The babysitters were the only ones who cared. So please, dad, don't even go there," Liya spat, rising to her feet in agitation.

Mrs. Bashara, with a confused look on her face, spoke, "Yes we were absent at times but we were working to get you everything that you have now. We worked really hard to give you both the best life. And mind you, your father and I have been trying so hard to make up for all that lost time for the past four years. We have both changed jobs and we're always here for you, so please Aliyah, that's not even a fair point," her mom said, walking towards them as she wiped her hands on her apron, wet from doing the dishes.

Liya spoke of a time years ago when the Bashara's were a struggling family and both parents were working really hard at making their home a decent one not just for them, but for their daughters–a feat which they have not only now achieved but surpassed. During those years, Mira and Liya remain under the care of babysitters and nannies.

Although their parents were only gone a few years before everything returned to normal, the girls preferred, for whatever reason, to use this as an excuse to disobey their parents.

"Look, my dears, we are your parents. We love you and want to be a part of your life. You can always come to us if you have any trouble or just need to talk, but please don't take out your anger or frustrations on your classmates or your teachers. Good children shouldn't do that," Mrs. Bashara said softly as she stood beside her husband, sitting at the end of the dining table with his head down as if in deep thought. Mrs. Bashara's long, curly, black hair which was usually bundled up in a scarf was now brushing gently against her husband's shoulders as she spoke but he didn't seem to mind.

"Whatever, mom. Let's go upstairs, Mira," Liya said with a pout, dragging her sister from the edge of her chair. Mira appeared to have been a little touched by her mom's words, but as soon as she felt Liya's hand grab her, all feelings of remorse dissolved.

"Today your principal said you almost got a suspension," Mr Bashara finally said in a very calm voice causing his daughters to stop in their tracks, "do you know what that means? By the way, do you know how that would look if both of the Bashara girls are suspended from school? You two are headed in that direction because this time girls, you've gone too far, and you have left me no choice.

You're grounded–both of you–until I see some positive changes in your attitude. From now on, you come home straight from school and that's final. If you defy these instructions, know that your punishment will just keep increasing."

"What? No! You can't ground me," Mira cried in a shrill voice.

"Oh yes I can," their father replied, nodding his head firmly. He didn't look like he was going to change his mind no matter what they said.

"Spring break begins in a few weeks. Surely you can't keep us locked in that whole time," Liya said, staring at her father in disbelief.

"That is totally up to you and you may go to your rooms now." he replied firmly, not looking up to meet her gaze.

The girls looked at one another with drooping shoulders, before turning towards the stairs. Mira's eyes were teary already. Liya, on the other hand, refused to show any emotion or "weakness". Instead she marched the polished wooden floor loudly with a stiff pout all the way to her room and slammed the door.

After the girls left the room, Mrs. Bashara moved a chair and sat close to her husband. Reaching out to hold his hands, and interceding on the twins behalf. They're just fifteen year olds, after all children make mistakes all the time, she said. But Mr. Bashara remained adamant about the girl's restrictions. He would not allow them to tarnish his family's name.

✳✳ ✳✳ ✳✳ ✳✳ ✳✳ ✳✳

"Good morning, honey," Mrs. Bashara said to Mira the next morning when she came down for breakfast. Mira, softly mumbling a greeting in reply as she took her seat.

Liya, on the other hand, walked down stairs and went past all of them, towards the door. Her hair, an unusual look with bold streaks of pink secured tightly in a bun, expected a comment from her father, but she was wrong because he didn't make a sound.

"Aliyah?" her mom called out from the table and she paused.

"Yeah?" she replied nonchalantly.

"You should sit down for breakfast," her mom said.

"I'm not hungry," She replied sharply.

"Well, you can at least wait for your sister," her mom added.

"She knows where to take the bus," Liya said.

"Liya?" her mom said, cajolingly.

Liya grumbled for a moment before she turned back and grabbed a chair to sit at the table. And with a smile, her mother served her breakfast of scrambled eggs and toast.

"So, your father and I had a lengthy discussion last night and your father has decided to renege on his decision to punish you. Haven't you, honey?" Mrs. Bashara said, looking up at her husband with a big, sweet, enticing smile and he grunted in reply, not looking up from his plate.

"So, we're not grounded for spring break any longer?" Mira asked, for clarity.

"Yes. But only on one condition," their mom said.

"Here we go," Liya said under her breath.

"We will all be going on a family camping trip together the first weekend of your spring break. We haven't spent much time together since you were little girls, so this should be fun," she explained excitedly.

"Eww, no. What sort of punishment is that?" Liya said out loud as her mom looked at her abruptly.

"It's not a punishment, Aliyah, it's a chance to redeem yourselves. What do you say, Mira? Would you rather spend your spring break locked in the house then?" Mrs. Bashara asked, and Mira shook her head.

"I didn't think so. So, talk to your sister. You have until tonight to give us your answer. And you'll get whatever you choose, really. So, choose wisely, girls," she said, peering at her watch to make sure she wasn't already running late for work before turning her attention back to her food.

The girls exchanged miserable glances and hurriedly finished their food. A weekend away with their parents would not be pleasant for them. They would have to be away from their friends and there would be lots of instructions and restrictions to follow and their freedom will be very

limited. This was something to think about
but they didn't have much of a choice.

CHAPTER TWO
A Plan

Time seemed to fly by quickly and before the twins knew it, the school semester was over and spring break had begun. The last day of school was usually everyone's happiest day. But for the girls, it was stressful because it only meant that the camping trip with their parents was drawing closer and they didn't want to think about it. So, there was no rush to get home. The twins decided to stall as much as possible by spending time at Laura's house with their friends before going home.

"I really don't want to go home," Mira said, slumping on the couch in Laura's house after their other friends left. Mira sat there staring at the white walls just as those in her own house but this house wasn't as big.

Laura Mill was the twins' closest friends-had been for a long time. And she was the queen of mischief. Her cute adorable blue eyes somehow always helped her get away with most of her mischievous behavior.

Mr. and Mrs. Bashara had often warned the girls against hanging out with the "blonde haired girl" as they called Laura, but the twins never listened.

Laura and her elder brother were their parents' only children just as it was with the Basharas. But unlike the twins, Laura didn't care anything about what her parents thought or said, and would often brag about how no one could tell her what to do. Her naughty behavior made her popular among the boys in school too. More than once, Mira and Liya wished in their hearts that they could exhibit Laura's behavior without consequences..

Liya grunted, joining her sister on the couch she replied, "I really don't want to go home either."

"Then don't," Laura said with an excited laugh, "there are tons of things we could do without ever getting bored. My silly brother will not be home anytime soon, and neither will my parents, so we have the rest of the day to ourselves. So let's get this party started, we could start off with a movie."

"I wish it was that easy. My dad threatened to intensify our punishments if we displayed any harsh behavior towards anyone again. So now we have to lay low and go on this silly camping trip as a family. Why did spring break have to come so quickly?" Liya groaned, looking sad and very unhappy.

"Oh my," Laura said, nodding her head, "that's sad, but it could still be fun if you want it to be."

"How, Laura? We will be so far away from all our friends and we'll have to always have our hair up in our hijab as mom always insists we do whenever we go to a new place. It will be so boorriinngg," Mira said, stretching out the last word much more than necessary.

"I have an idea but it will take a lot of courage. Do you want to hear it?" Laura said, with a glint of excitement in her eyes as she rubbed her palms together deviously.

"Sure," the twins said at the same time. Laura always had ideas up her sleeve and they were down for anything that would lessen the boredom that they assumed the coming weekend would bring.

Laura chuckled as she explained every detail of her malicious plan. "But to make this plan work it will take courage".

"Yes, it definitely does. Let's just think of something else," Mira replied with an uncomfortable laugh. She liked Laura's idea, but she wasn't that brave.

"Nope Mira, we will go with Laura's plan," Liya cut in. "What? Liya, no we can't-" Mira started to say but her sister interrupted her.

"Oh, don't be such a scaredy-cat. It's not even a big deal. We'll just give our parents a little scare, that's all. And it'll teach them a lesson so they can stop bothering us. Oh boy, I can imagine the look on dad's face when we perfectly execute Laura's plan," Liya said, laughing spitefully.

"Exactly. It worked on my parents and they stopped bugging me. It should work on yours too." Laura said with a satisfied smile.

"Thank you so much, Laura. I love you so much," Liya said, pulling the giggling Laura Mill into a very tight hug.

"Come on, Mira," Liya called out to her sister, who was still seated on the couch, staring into space. Clearly, Laura's plan unnerved her.

"Come on, chicken," Laura called out jeeringly and that brought Mira to her feet.

"I'm no chicken," she said defensively, walking over to form a group hug. Mira could stand to be called many things, but she hated being called a chicken, and they all knew that.

"Group hugs are nice," Laura said, burying her head in between their shoulders.

"So what will you be doing this weekend?" Mira asked Laura after they separated from the embrace.

"Planning a party. I was hoping you both could join me but since you will be away, it's totally fine."

"I'm so sorry," Liya said as her face fell in disappointment.

"Don't worry. I'll be getting all of us tickets anyway, so you will be attending for sure. Just have yourselves a fun weekend and I expect to receive exciting tales when you return," Laura said with a big smile.

"Yes indeed. You can count on that," Liya said with glee.

"We have to leave now though," Mira said, grabbing her backpack.

"Hey, relax," Laura said softly, holding her hand.

"My sister is right. We've got to leave now. We don't know for certain what our dad could have up his sleeve again," Liya added, also grabbing her backpack from a chair, "Bye, Laura."

"Bye, girls," Laura replied in a sing-song voice as she followed them to lock the door.

** ** ** ** **

It was a windy Friday afternoon. The girls watched as their mom double checked everything they placed inside the family van making sure they didn't leave anything behind. Standing there as the wind played with her purple hijab and the writing pad in her hands, she checked off everything on her lists.

"I think it might rain honey," Mrs. Bashara called out loudly so her husband could hear from inside the house.

They were expected to leave for their cabin much earlier in the day, but Mr. Bashara suddenly had a work-related emergency to handle. Despite his claim that he was almost done, he was still sitting at the dinner table typing loudly away on his laptop. The delay was annoying and the girls were becoming impatient.

While waiting for Mr. Bashara to complete his work, Mrs. Bashara explained the details of their destination. It was going to be at a cabin on one of their father's properties a few hours away. Their mom went on and on about how beautiful it usually is in that area during spring and how much they would enjoy the scenery and the flowers. She was so excited as she talked about how they would take plenty of lovely photos and try out some new recipes.

Mrs. Bashara said that there would be no use of phones or gadgets throughout the weekend either, which was the reason they were still at home waiting for their father to finish working.

"What do you mean no phones?" Mira asked, with a look of horror after their mom finished giving out rules and instructions.

"It means exactly what I said it means baby. The signal in the camping area is quite poor anyway, so you won't be needing your electronics," Mrs. Bashara replied.

Liya remained silent, asking no questions. As far as she was concerned, she and her sister had no intention of staying long in the cabin anyway and she wondered why Mira was asking questions in the first place.

By the time their father was done with his work, it was evening. And contrary to their mother's prediction, it still hadn't rained. Mr. Bashara apologized to them and insisted they continue with the trip of the day. He pointed out that if night fell along the way, they would stop at a hotel, rest and start their travels again at the break of day. It is going to be so much more fun this way, he said.

With Mr. Bashara behind the wheel of the family van, Mrs. Bashara to his right, and the girls sitting on the second row seats in the back, all holding their matching blue hijabs which their mom insisted that they carry as they are enjoying the cool music playing from the car stereo.

In the course of the drive, the parents tried to include the twins in their conversations more than once, but the twins showed no interest and kept giving monosyllabic answers every time they asked a question. After their failed attempt to communicate with the twins, they gave up altogether.

Despite the communication blunder, Mrs. Bashara maintained her happy demeanor because she still believed that the results of this trip will bring about that bond her family so desperately needs.

"How much farther is the place?" Mira asked, since they had been driving for about four hours.

"We're almost there," her mom replied, reassuringly.

"It's getting late though," Mira muttered under her breath. She had never been a fan of long drives and travels. She hated having to sit in one spot for any length of time.

After driving for a while longer, Mr. Bashara asked his wife to search for a good hotel because it was time to retire for the evening. As they drove into the hotel's premises, Mira sighed loudly in relief.

Once inside the hotel lobby, Liya let her eyes wander. The place was huge but the design was quite simple, yet fascinating. While their parents checked in with the hotel clerk, Liya continued to feed her eyes, taking in the golden lights and the polished furniture which gave the lobby an old antique appearance. It was fascinating.

Just as Liya was admiring the structured art and about to mark her territory so she wouldn't be lost when she finally decided to–

"Aliyah?" Her mom's voice called, breaking into her reverie, "are you not coming?" Liya looked up to find that the rest of her family were already walking ahead of her so she picked up her pace and followed.

The parents checked the twins into their suite making sure they were safe and secure, then they left for their own.

Being sure that her parents had left, Liya tiptoed out of their suite while Mira was in the bathroom. She checked to see if her parents were settled in their suite so she wouldn't get caught.

The door to their suite was open a little so she peeked in, finding both her parents catching up on their *Isha* prayers. She breathed out a sigh of relief. "Great!" She quietly closed the door and softly made her way to the elevator.

** ** ** ** **

The hotel attendant, smiling and showing his badge to identify himself, rolled the large food trolley into the twins suite. Mira was ecstatic because she was going crazy with hunger.

"Thank you," Mr. Bashara said as the attendant placed the trays on the tables then made his way out of the suite with the trolley.

"Alright Amirah. Call your sister. It's time to eat," Mrs. Bashara said.

"Aliyah? She's not in the room. I thought she was with you," Mira said.

"Huh-no way," Mrs. Bashara replied, confusion crossing her face as she rose to her feet.

"Check again. Perhaps she's in the bathroom," Mr. Bashara said calmly.

Amirah gave a shrug and went back into their room to see if Aliyah was just being difficult and hiding somewhere, but after checking every inch of the suite, Aliyah wasn't anywhere to be found, so she started to worry.

"I can't find her, dad," she said in a high-pitched voice as she walked into the main room.

"Oh my God!" her mom exclaimed, hitting her palm on her forehead as she tried not to think of all the possible dangers Aliyah could be facing.

Just as she said that, the door knob turned and a smiling Aliyah tiptoed into the suite but as she saw her parents face, her smile vanished and she stood up straight.

"You made us worried Aliyah! Where did you go? I asked you to remain in your rooms," Mr. Bashara said in a stern voice.

"I just went out for a bit. I wanted to look around the hotel, that's all," she replied indifferently.

"Do you have any idea how–,"her father started to say in a raised voice but her mom reached out to hold his arm, prompting him to calm down.

"You should have told your sister at least, Aliyah. Just don't ever scare us like that again," her mom said calmly, "now let's eat."

Mr. Bashara looked like he wanted to say more, but he restrained himself and let his wife handle the situation. They were on a quest to become closer to their children and raising his voice would only make matters worse.

After dinner, everyone had calmed down, their parents once again watched the twins go into their room, leaving them with strict instructions to actually stay in their suite this time.

As soon as their parents left the suite, Liya couldn't wait to talk about her adventure. "Mira, I've been able to survey the area and it's not going to be difficult for us to get out of this hotel and get a taxi," Liya said.

"What are you talking about?" Mira asked, confused.

"Huh–the plan was to escape, remember?" Liya pointed out to her sister, rolling her eyes.

"I thought we had forgotten about that. Camping could actually be fun, you know?" Mira said.

"What do you mean?" Liya scoffed, "did you forget that it's a punishment, sister? One we got in exchange for getting grounded. You agreed to our escape plan back at Laura's house so what's the problem now?"

"No problem, just thinking, maybe we should give this camping trip a shot." Mira replied hesitantly. As much as she liked the idea of an adventure just like her sister, she just wasn't feeling it this time.

"So, we'll leave very early in the morning. I'll set an alarm," Liya said conclusively but Mira said nothing.

** ** ** ** **

As soon as Mrs. Bashara was done with her morning prayers, she walked over to the girls' suite to wake them. It was a cold morning and it was still early. Mrs Bashara was a little reluctant to knock on their door, but how could she expect them to take their prayers seriously if no one encouraged them?

When the twins were very young, Mrs. Bashara trained them to pray and she always looked at them with pride whenever she saw their little figures bowing down for prayers. She smiled at the memory. But in reality, that's all it was, just a memory.

During her brief period of absence from their lives the twins had grown and they had changed. Prayer wasn't important to them anymore. She sighed deeply as she mustered the patience she needed to deal with them. They were going to give her trouble, she knew it, but she was determined to handle them with kitten gloves.

She turned the knob slowly and entered into the twins' suite. Just enough light washed in from the drapes to find the light switch and turn on the light. As she moved toward the girl's bed, she stopped in her tracks. She expected grunts, she expected grumbling at the flip of the switch, but what she didn't expect were empty beds. The twins were gone.

"Honey?!" she yelled, calling for her husband's attention as worry flooded her heart and she fell upon their bed.

"Yes dear?" Mr. Bashara replied from the doorway. He had just gone into the bathroom when his wife called. Hurrying to put his shirt back on, he rushed to her aid.

Assuming something was terribly wrong with the twins, he ran into their room. Immediately he understood why his wife had yelled. The beds before him—the beds that belonged to his daughters—were well made and the girls were nowhere in sight. How is this possible? Where in the world were his daughters?

CHAPTER THREE
The Cursed Book

"What should we do next?" Liya asked in excitement as she downed the rest of her ice cream in a rush.

"I don't know," Mira replied glumly. She was also eating ice cream but unlike her sister, she ate hers slowly, without much enthusiasm.

"Come on, Mira. What is it with your mood swings? You were over the top just a few seconds ago," Liya uttered in frustration as she kicked her legs against the ground.

After they escaped from their parents in the earlier hours of that morning, they explored as much of the small town as they possibly could. Because of their status and allowances. money wasn't a problem. The mini-mall, the pool, the diners the locals called "the best", and the "famous" ice cream shop, they were having a swell day trying every cool spot they heard the locals talk about. But soon there wasn't much else to see in the small town, so they just sat on a long benche in the nearby park continuing to gulp down their ice cream.

"I was pulling your legs, Liya. Of course, I'm happy," Mira said, replacing her frown with a bright smile as she dug into her ice cream again.

"Great," her sister replied, filled with glee again, "perhaps we should check out the-"

"Bookstore next," Mira chipped in, clapping her hands in childish enthusiasm.

"No. That sounds a little boring," Liya said, dismissing it with a wave of her hand.

Mira's face slowly folded into an ugly frown, and she folded her arms across her chest in defiance.

"I've followed you everywhere you wanted to go all day, so now I'm going over to the bookstore; with or without you sister." She said point-blank.

"There are tons of other fun places we could check out. Books are like-so not it," Liya retorted.

"Like where?" Mira asked, widening her eyes. "Where, Liya?" She asked again when her sister didn't reply, "see?"

"Alright. Alright. Bookstore it is. But we won't be spending a lot of time there," Liya surrendered. "Whatever!" said Mira

The twins walked hand in hand to the bookstore that caught Mira' eye earlier in the day. Just a few blocks from the Ice Cream Parlor.

"Do you think our parents are worried about us?" Mira asked abruptly along the way. "I guess they'll be a little worried, " Liya replied with a shrug, "but what does it matter, anyway? They deserve to feel bad, Mira. So don't start with the pity party. Did you forget, they wanted to ground us, remember?" Mira did not reply. She just nodded slowly in reluctant agreement.

"Hey, look. We're almost there," Liya announced, pointing towards the bookstore a few steps ahead, and she watched in satisfaction as her sister's face lit up.

Soon enough, they heard the little doorbell jingle as they walked into the small bookstore. And much to Liya's surprise, the book store was packed with more people than she could have imagined.

"I didn't know people loved books this much," she muttered under her breath. "Told you. You're the odd one out," Mira replied quietly as she dashed off to a section of the book store that caught her attention, "I'll see you soon, sister." And with that, she slipped away.

** ** ** ** **

Liya peeked in between the shelves in search of her sister. They had been in the bookstore for quite a while, and it seemed like they were the only ones left, but her quest was to find Mira.

"Girl, I've been looking for you everywhere," Liya said impatiently when she finally found Mira crouched down beside a shelf, admiring a book at the far end of the bookstore. "Liya," Mira said breathily as she looked up with a smile. "We should get going," Liya said, reaching out to pull her up.

"By the way, Liya, I saw this book with an attractive cover in the children's section that got my attention. Let me show you. It has this creepy but alluring feel that I can't exactly describe and I can't remember the title, but–"

"You mean, *Old slave tales?*" A deep voice interrupted from behind them, making them jump.

"Y–yes. That's it, I think," Mira said, turning around to see who the bearer of the voice was.

"I'm sorry, girls. I didn't mean to scare you," the old man said, spreading his lips into a warm, homely smile, "I'm Smith. The kids around here call me Mr. Smith, and I own this store. It's nice to meet you."

Mr. Smith was an older man. He had wrinkled skin and receding white hair that looked very much like fine silk. And as he spoke, he kept adjusting his wire-rimmed glasses that just kept slipping down to his nose. When he wasn't doing that, he was wiping his hands against his waist apron.

"It's nice to meet you too. I'm Mira, and this is my twin sister, Liya," Mira said, "How did you know what book I was referring to, though?"

Mr. Smith smiled again.

"Many children who come here get intrigued at the sight of that book. You're not the first. So, I recognized that look in your eyes. But that book is not for sale."

"It's not?" Mira asked, widening her eyes.

"No, it isn't. It's an old folklore, so I prefer to keep it here.Occasionally, I let a few trusted people borrow it from time to time," Mr Smith explained.

"That's nice," Mira said.

At that moment, Liya tugged at her sister's arm, urging her to round off her conversation.

"Do you want to hear the story, perhaps? I'm a pretty great narrator," Mr. Smith said with a soft chuckle.

"Yes! Of course," Mira replied hastily but paused as she turned to look at her sister, "I mean, I'll have to talk to my sister first."

"Alright, girls, if you're still interested, I'll be at the counter," he said softly as he turned to walk away.

"I want to hear the story," Mira said to her sister as soon as Mr. Smith left.

"Who says I don't want to, either?" Liya asked, placing her hands on her waist.

"Oh really," Miya chuckled. She expected an argument at the very least.

"Come on. The old man's waiting," Liya reminded her. And together, they walked over to the counter, eager to find out what is so special about this book.

"Haha! I see you've decided to stay for the story. Would you like some tea?" Mr. Smith asked as he pulled out stools for them.

"No, thank you. We're fine," Liya answered for them both. She was curious about the story too, but she wasn't a big fan of strangers.

"Alright then," Mr. Smith said, moving to sit on his stool right in front of the girls, "you should call your parents and let them know where you are and that you'll be coming in late, though; this might take a while."

"There will be no need for that, sir," Liya replied sharply, "Please, let's get on with the story."

Mira turned to glare at her sister as Mr. Smith had seemed taken aback by her speech, and Liya mouthed, "what?"

"Alright then," Mr. Smith said, putting back on his warm smile as he handed the book over to the girls so they could follow along and check out the pictures in the book.

"I shall start from the very beginning. Fasten your belts, ladies," he announced.

"Long ago, in the time when slaves were rampant and there were signs that labeled families as influential. There lived a slave named Franzel. This slave was smart, obedient, and did everything exactly as his master instructed.

He was talented and skilled at many things. He could cook, clean and serve his master with the efficiency and speed of a machine. But his master was a hard man who had a naughty son.

The master could not trust any other servant to be his son's servant, so he chose Franzel. But secretly, the other slaves were happy because this master's son was truly a difficult young boy. He ordered Franzel around and play pranks on him whenever he liked, but Franzel remained a loyal slave who only did what was right.

One day, after the Master scolded his son for wrongdoings, this young boy threw a "mighty tantrum".You can't even imagine the things he did?"

"What did he do?" The girls asked simultaneously with rapt attention.

"He ran away from home." Mr. Smith replied with disapproval in his eyes.

The girls shifted uncomfortably in their chairs as Mr. Smith cleared his throat before going on with his story.

"The master was livid when he found out. He turned the house over and lashed out at all the servants, threatening to kill them all if they didn't find his son. The rest of the slaves quickly excluded themselves from blame, pushing Franzel forward as he was supposed to be the boy's keeper.

When the first night passed, and the young boy still hadn't been found, the master turned all of his frustration and anger towards Franzel, depriving him of food and spewing heavy threats. When on the third night, the young master, as the slaves called him, still wasn't in his room, the father had Franzel bound up and flogged mercilessly. Then he asked that blades from his garden shed be brought to him and sharpened.

With every passing hour, he chopped off chunks of Franzel's right leg, beginning with his toes. At first, the blood dripped in trickles and then it began to gush out. Franzel was in horrible, unimaginable pain.

But the master was the least concerned. All that mattered to the Master was that his son was found, so all of Franzel's cries (about truly not knowing the boy's whereabouts) fell on deaf ears. As I said earlier, the master was a hard man, and he always did what he wanted."

"Eww. That's disgusting," Liya exclaimed, making a sick face, and Mr. Smith smiled.

"So, what happened next?" Mira asked, still appearing to be lost in the story. She moved the book from the desk as if she was going to read it herself. Mr. Smith sighed and stared into space.

"Finally, the young master returned home the very next day after he was satisfied with all of his escapades with his friends. When he ran out of money, he decided to go back home but a day too late of Franzel's near demise.

Mira gasped, "But what about Franzel?"

"He was but a slave, after all. Slaves were not allowed to do anything to defend themselves against the Master.

The master ordered the nurse to bandaged Franzel's wounds, and ordered the other slaves to carry out his duties until he was better. When he returned to continue his duties in his master's house, he was left with just one leg. Franzel's life changed forever. He couldn't do any tedious physical work so he was confined to the kitchen. He grew to resent Junior and every child who was disobedient and didn't listen to their parents instructions.

He never had children of his own because he thought of them as "bundles of mischief". Although, Franzel is long dead, it is said that his ghost still said haunts children like Junior (selfish, rude) who refuse to listen to their parents and who pull worrisome stunts like running away from home," Mr. Smith continued.

At that moment, pure fright filled the girls' hearts. Why was Mr. Smith talking like he knew what they had done just that morning?

"And what does this ghost do when he comes across those children?" Mira asked with widened eyes.

"The story has it that he follows them around, making their lives a living horror, but they won't be able to see him. Instead, children will smell the strong stench that comes from him, the stench of old, dry, metallic blood as of a steel mill. His ghost flashes as a warning smoke, to warn these children to change their ways. But if they choose to remain disobedient, Franzel follows them closely and will not stop until they are punished as he was by his master, chopping off their legs from their toes up," he said.

Liya was beginning to tremble in her chair as she imagined her toes being chopped off. She looked up at Mr. Smith's face in fear, and he laughed softly.

"Did I mention that all children who have had encounters with Franzel the ghost are always found with streaks of gray hair as a receipt?" said Mr. Smith as he rubbed his fingers against his chin in thought.

"Gray hair?" Liya asked, her horror intensifying.

"When the ghost of Franzel touches you, your hair will turn gray. But if he catches you, he will chop off your leg as the slave master did him. Those were the exact words in the book," Mr. Smith finishing the book with a warm smile, was starting to make the twins feel even more uncomfortable.

"But of course, only troublesome children have to worry about the ghost of Franzel and I don't think you two are in that category. Are you?" he asked, rising from his chair.

The girls were transfixed to their seats. The story left them spooked, and they couldn't bring themselves to say a word.

"Our time is far spent," Mr. Smith said, peering at his wristwatch, "we should all get going. It's way past my closing time, but it was nice sharing the story with you. You may come back anytime you want."

"Let's go," Liya whispered to her sister as she nudged her.

"Okay," Mira said in agreement as she rose to her feet too. She packed her things, and together they walked out of the bookstore, not taking another look back at Mr. Smith, who didn't seem to mind either.

They walked the next few blocks in silence until they arrived at the park where they had been seated earlier, and made their way to a bench. It was evening already.

"What is that in your hand?" Liya asked her sister as soon as they settled on the bench.

Mira looked at the book she was holding and let out a small cry. She had forgotten to return the book to Mr. Smith before they left.

"I completely forgot," she said with a deep sigh. She placed the book in the space between her and her sister and examined it again, wondering why she found it attractive in the first place. Now, that creepy alluring book cover just looks ordinary, like a regular children's book.

"We should return it," Mira pointed out.

"Yes, we should," Liya said, sounding more lighthearted than before, "you know what else we should do? We should forget about this dumb tale and stop looking like we've seen this "Francis" ghost or whatever. I mean, look at this book. It's just another one of those stupid stories naïve kids believe."

It sounded like she was still trying to convince herself, and Mira sure did need the encouragement.

"True," Mira replied.

"You see this is foolishness, why don't we drop by the ice cream shop again and have a great time? The book store will be closed by now anyway, and we could just give it back anytime. It's not our fault that he left the book with us anyway," Liya added.

"That sounds like a plan," Mira said, feeling a little perky.

As soon as they rose from the bench, a strong, ugly stench wafted past Mira's nose.

"What's that smell?" She asked, cupping her hands around her nose as she looked around to see what must have brought that odor.

"What smell?" Liya asked, looking up at her.

"I don't know. It smells so gross, like-" Mira paused as the odor drifted towards them again, and this time, Liya smelled it too.

"Like- metal," Liya said.

"Y-yes," Mira said slowly as fear crept into her chest again.

"It can't possibly be-," she started to say, but her sister cut in.

"Don't start thinking about that crazy story, Mira. That smell is probably from a house in the area or something. It can't be anything serious."

Liya managed to convince Mira, but when the smell wouldn't go away, even Liya started to panic.

"I think we should just go back to mum and dad," Mira suggested, and her sister didn't need much convincing.

All their thoughts of ice cream were forgotten, the twins headed back to the hotel where their family had lodged the night before.

CHAPTER FOUR

Changes

Mrs. Bashara's puffy eyes widened as soon as she saw her girls walk back into the suite, where she was sprawled on a couch. She had been crying.

"Alhamdulillah," she exclaimed, as she jumped to her feet, ran over to the girls and threw her arms around them, almost choking them. The book in Mira's hands clattered to the ground.

"Oh, my babies, where have you been?" she asked through sniffles, still not unclutching her arms off them. Then suddenly she remembered that the girls had committed an unjust offense, so she pulled away abruptly.

"You girls have a lot of explaining to do to your father and me. Where have you been all day?!" she asked as she placed her hands on her hips.

The doorknob turned just then, and they heard Mr. Bashara's voice. He was having a conversation with another man at the door.

"Great. Your father is here. Start preparing your explanation, and it better be good."

The men walked into the room, still deep in their discussion, which seemed to be about the girls. As soon as Mr. Bashara saw his daughters, he paused in his tracks. "Oh thank goodness," he said under his breath.

"You must be Aliyah and Amirah," the second man said, flashing a relieved smile. He was a tall, big man and his deep voice resonated the room as he spoke, "I'm Mr. Greene, the manager of this hotel. I told you they would be found, Mr. Bashara. This town is relatively small. One cannot so easily disappear."

He looked very relieved. The fact that two girls had disappeared from his hotel must have borne a lot of stress on him. The Bashara's were rich people, and no one ever wants to be on the wrong side of wealthy people. If word had gotten out about the incident, the reputation of the hotel's security would undoubtedly have been dented.

"Thank you for everything, Mr. Greene," Mr. Bashara said, extending his hand for a handshake, paying no mind to his daughters at all. He wore a straight face, but he was so angry, and the girls knew that.

"Oh, it's fine, Mr. Bashara. I'm glad you have your children back. Please do not hesitate to reach out again if you need anything else. Enjoy the rest of your stay. *Assalamu alaikum,*" he said with a slight amusing bow. On sensing the awkward tension in the room and seeing that no one recognized his humor, he cleared his throat and let himself out.

As soon as Mr. Greene left, the room became hushed. The girls remained still in the middle of the room, shifting from foot to foot with their gazes fixed on the gleaming white floor tiles. Mrs. Bashara returned to the couch, and her husband joined her.

"Go on, ladies, I'm all ears," He said in a very calm voice. He was barely audible.

"Come on, say something. You've been away all-day having fun, haven't you? Or at least that's what your mum's purse says. Correct me if I'm wrong. You could have at least taken your phone, but no, you didn't think of that. It didn't matter to you that anything could have happened to you out there, and we wouldn't know anything about it. It didn't even matter to you that we're all in an unfamiliar town and you could have gotten lost. All that you care about is yourself. What were you thinking?"

Liya shrugged nonchalantly in response, and that infuriated her father.

"No, Aliyah, you're not allowed to do that. You are wrong, and you should apologize. That's what you should be doing right now," Mrs. Bashara chided as she reached to hold her husband's hand.

"We were on the verge of calling the police, girls. I was so scared, and your father was so worried. We combed the entire hotel looking for you, and I've barely tasted anything all day.

I don't know why you did this thing after you saw the effect on us last night, but this behavior crosses the line. You went way too far this time and I don't even know what to say," she added.

"If you hadn't forced us to follow you on this stupid trip, no one would have had to run away. Isn't that right, Mira?" Liya commented obstinately.

Mira only nodded slowly with her gaze still fixed to the ground, and Mrs. Bashara's face fell.

"What did you just say?" Mr. Bashara replied loudly as he rose to his feet. He knew how much this trip meant to his wife. It was the only reason he agreed to it in the first place. Left up to him, he'll have the girls grounded back at home till they come to their right minds.

"You had a choice. Your mum gave you an option, but you chose the trip of your own accord. So, don't start playing the victim. Where did you even get this silly idea that throwing tantrums are the solutions to issues? For God's sake, girls, you are not toddlers anymore. You can't just do whatever you like when you want and expect us to take it-"he added in a heated voice. Finding his daughters' attitudes very irritating.

"Oh, please, dad. Stop making this a big deal. We are back now, aren't we? So why are you yelling? You and mum need to let us breathe, okay? You need to stop-" Liya paused as the ugly stench they had perceived earlier swarmed the room. It was a heavy metallic stink that instantly brought back to the girls' mind the story that Mr. Smith told them.

"What is wrong with you?" Mr. Bashara asked, squinting his eyes. He was clearly offended.

Mira finally raised her head and slowly turned to look at her sister's face.

"Franzel," she whispered with fear in her eyes. Liya wanted to deny it and tell her sister that it was pure foolishness. Oooh, she wanted to so badly, but she couldn't. The stench was pungent all through the room; there was no denying it. And she could only think of one explanation. If only they hadn't stayed back to listen to that stupid story.

"You shouldn't speak to your father that way, Aliya," Mrs. Bashara said as she began to walk towards them.

The girls continued to exchange glances, not paying attention to their parents. The stench was becoming even more intense, and it was suffocating. Liya began to cough.

"We-we're sorry!" Mira rambled, "I mean, I admit that we were wrong, and we're sorry. It won't happen again."

Right after the apology, the air was pure again, and Liya's cough ceased. She panted for the next few seconds, trying to catch her breath.

Mrs. Bashara sighed and stared at both of them for a moment. Her gaze lingered on Liya the longest, and she shook her head. As far as she was concerned, the coughing fit had been fake, intended to change the conversation's direction. But who could blame her? It was a stunt Liya could very well pull.

"It's been a long day for all of us. We should get some sleep," Mrs. Bashara said calmly.

"All of us," she said again as she turned to her husband, who still had his eyes angrily fixed on the girls.

Mr. Bashara nodded in agreement and gave his wife a small smile before he turned to go into the suite he shared with his wife.

"Good night, girls," Mrs. Bashara said before following her husband.

"Mum, wait," Mira whispered.

"Yes?"

"Will we still be going to dad's resort tomorrow?" she asked cautiously.

"I don't know. It was supposed to be for a weekend, and we've just wasted a whole day here. Let's wait till tomorrow morning and see what your father has to say," she replied with a slight smile. She wasn't very pleased with the events of the day.

"Alright," Mira said softly as she played absentmindedly with her fingers. Mrs. Bashara nodded and continued on to join her husband.

As soon as their door was closed, Mira glanced at her sister, who still looked pale from all the coughing.

"Hey, are you alright?" Mira asked, placing her arm around Liya's shoulder.

"I think this ghost story could be true," Liya replied, staring into space. Mira could not disagree, and the very fact that Liya believed it too unnerved her even more.

"What should we do?" Liya asked as she turned to face Mira, "what do we do if the ghost comes for us?"

"It won't come for us," Mira reassured.

"But what if?" she asked again.

According to the story, all we have to do is listen to mum and dad's instructions, remember? So that's what we'll do," Mira answered.

"We shouldn't have gone to that bookstore, Mira. We shouldn't have listened when he offered to narrate the story to us, and now we've even brought the stupid, cursed book home with us. We should have just thrown it away," Liya wailed.

For the first time in a long time, Mira saw her sister admitting her fears and this time; she knew she had to act as the brave one.

"Come on, Liya. We'll be fine. Let's just sleep, and maybe when we wake up tomorrow, things might be different. Who knows?" Mira suggested, "Let's go to bed, sister." as she dragged Liya along to their beds.

Despite the events of the day and all that they had on their minds, they both got a good night's sleep because their bodies needed the rest.

Hopefully, today's experience had an impact on them so much that they will wake up the next morning as different and more obedient children.

The next morning, the Bashara family woke up late-including the parents-but they all felt refreshed and alive. Even Mr. Bashara seemed to be in a better mood.

"Good morning, ladies," He greeted the twins, as soon as they came out for breakfast.

"Good morning, dad. Good morning, mum," they replied simultaneously.

"Good morning, girls," Mrs. Baker replied, beaming.

The twins didn't talk much throughout breakfast. They looked lightened-serene and remorseful.

I hope you two didn't fully unpack your bags because we will be checking out shortly," Mr. Bashara announced as soon as they finished breakfast.

"Are we going back home now?" Mira asked, looking up at her father.

"And let all of our planning go to waste? No, no. Of course not," Mr. Bashara said heartily,

"We will continue on our trip as we've planned. We will just spend a few extra days in the cabin, that's all," Mrs. Bashara explained.

"That's right," Mr. Bashara chipped in, "So, go on ahead and pack up. There's no need to waste anymore time here."

The atmosphere was homely and fresh, and the twins were confused because their parents were acting like they hadn't just troubled them the day before.

"Go on," Mrs. Bashara said again, flashing a big, sweet smile their way to push them.

"Yes, mum," Mira replied.

Liya said little to nothing all morning, and Mira could tell that she was still in thought.

"Hey, I know you're worried about–" Mira started to say as they packed their bags in their room.

"No, I'm not. I'm fine," Liya cut in, smiling brightly.

"You are?" Mira asked. Her sister didn't look "fine" to her. Silence had never been Liya's thing. She always had something to say about everything–

"Yes, I am Mira. Let's just say getting a good night's sleep helped calm me down," she reassured.

"Alright then," Mira replied as she zipped up her bag.

"Camping," Liya said under her breath while zipping up her bag.

"Should be fun," Mira said with a bright smile.

"I hope so," her sister replied. Walking out to meet their parents, who were all set themselves. "Everything good?" Mr. Bashara asked, and they all nodded.

As they drove out of the hotel parking lot, their father began to play soft music, the events of the past few days washed through Mira's mind, and she could guess it was what Liya was thinking about too while staring out the window.

They only intended to stay one night in that town, but there they were, leaving more than twenty-four hours later. Mira's mind went back to all the places she'd explored with her sister, and she smiled. But as her memory was filled with the bookstore part, her smile became weaker.

She searched the bottom of her bag making sure she had the cursed book in there. She hated that she was carrying it along with them, and she knew that Liya would most probably throw a fit. She had thoughts of leaving it behind at the hotel but she knew it would be trashed and something just wouldn't let her leave it.

Mr. Smith told them he liked to keep the book on his shelf for visitors to see. It was only right that she looked for a way to get it back to him.

Franzel's name flashed in her head, and she shivered. Thinking if they could find a way to get rid of the book, maybe the ghost would be gone forever.

But for the moment, Mira and her twin sister would have to find a way to enjoy this short vacation with their parents and hope they all have a great time. After all, they really didn't have much of a choice. She just hoped that the resort would be a fun place.

CHAPTER FIVE
A New Leaf

Liya bounced on her springy bed and felt the cool, soft white sheets embrace her. The rest of the trip to her resort had been short and blissful. Even the cabin had a peaceful appeal. The scenery was incredible.

Whoever it was that her father paid to do the gardening had done a perfect job. Flowers of different colors and beautiful chirping birds were all over the place, and it greatly complimented the small, wooden brown cabin. Altogether, it gave a serene, picturesque appeal. She had to admit.

"It's having an effect on you too, isn't it?" Mira asked from the doorway. Liya hadn't heard the door when Mira opened it. Everything was quiet in the cabin, down to the doors.

"What is?" Liya asked, raising her head.

"Nature, tranquility. I know you feel it too," Mira replied as she walked over to sit on her sister's bed.

"Doesn't change the fact that we don't want to be here," Liya commented quietly but Mira said nothing.

"What is your room like?" Liya asked, lightening the mood.

The cabin was small, but it had three rooms, enough for the girls to have separate rooms, just like it was at home. "Just like this one. It's the same color too," Mira replied.

Everything in the house had the same sheen that came with polished wood.

"Wow, that's amazing," Liya said. And the room went quiet again. Unsure of what to do next, Mira stared down at her fingers which she was twirling around on her lap.

Just then, their mum beckoned them from the living room. Mira rose immediately to answer the call but paused when she found that her sister hadn't moved.

"Mum called our names," Mira pointed out. "I know," Liya replied quietly, not looking at her sister.

"You're not coming?" Mira asked. "No, I'm not."

"Huh-" Mira said as she tried to find the right way to remind her sister about Franzel.

"I brought the book along with me," she finally announced, clearing her throat. Those words alone forced Liya into a sitting position.

"The cursed book?" Liya asked.

"Yes. So we both need to answer mum like right now," Mira pointed out cautiously.

Liya grunted loudly, "Why did you-?" she started to say, but Mrs. Bashara's voice interrupted her.

"We're coming!" Liya bellowed and marched out of the room with Mira following closely behind her.

"We're sorry, we were settling some of our stuff," Mira apologized as soon as they walked into the living room. Mrs. Bashara looked up at them and smiled.

"Oh, that's fine. I'm just glad you like this place," she said as she laid some bowls on the table in the center of the room, just in front of the fireplace.

"No one says we do," Liya grumbled under her breath as she bounced onto the sofa.

"Liya? Franzel!" Mira whispered sharply, correcting her. It appeared that the thought of the steel mill stench lingered more in Mira's mind than in her sister's.

"What I mean is," Liya paused to clear her throat, "Yes, we love this place. The scenery is just perfect. I didn't know we had such a lavish vacation home."

"Yeah, I know," Mrs. Bashara said, beaming as she crouched to place a chilled bowl of fruit salad at the center of the table, "It's why I suggested that we come here. Your father loves to invest in property, and it's admirable."

"So, are there other ones just like this one?" Liya asked.

"Of course. You can spend every spring break throughout high school in different ones," Mrs. Bashara replied with a small laugh.

"You never ask these things," she said softly, turning from the snack set up she was making on the table to look at Liya briefly. There was surprise in her eyes.

"Wow," Mira said as she moved to sit beside her sister.

"There's a lake a few meters away from the cabin, by the way," Mrs. Bashara added with a glint in her eyes, "you and your sister could go check it out later. It's a lovely sight. You could take my camera along. Trust me; you won't regret it."

"Yeah, sure," Mira said gleefully.

"But first, you should go wash your hands and get your father. I spent a lot of time preparing these snacks," Mrs. Bashara said as she rose to her feet. She rubbed her palms against her thighs as she admired the table.

Liya thought it was funny, and she chuckled. She had never seen her mum stare at food like that before, so it amused her.

"Come on, girls, get up," their mum said.

"I'll go get dad," Liya said cheerily.

"Handwashing, it is then," Mira said.

Mrs. Bashara stared in amazement at her children as they walked away to do as she had instructed. Had Aliya just opted to do something without having to be coerced?

Later that night, when the girls turned in, Mrs. Bashara sat with her husband in front of the fireplace, sipping sweet wine as she reminisced on all the events of the day.

"Coming here was a great idea," she said softly as she smiled to herself.

"I agree," Mr. Bashara replied with a smile.

"I mean, I don't know what came over our kids but they have been acting so weird," she chuckled, "did you say something to Aliya after we left the hotel?"

"Nope, not a word," her husband replied with a shrug.

"Alright," she said hesitantly. It could be the effect of a guilty conscience.

"Perhaps, our prayers for them are finally being answered," Mr. Bashara said as he refilled both their glasses.

"Perhaps," Mrs. Bashara said, beaming as she clinked her glass against her husband's, "Cheers".

Mrs. Bashara still wasn't sure what it was that came over her kids, but she was grateful for whatever it was, so she whispered a short prayer in gratitude.

If the girls could continue in the same spirit, it would make her happy. She sincerely hoped that things would stay the way they were today, and that it wasn't all a dream.

** ** ** ** **

The following day, Mr. and Mrs. Bashara woke up to find that the girls were already up. The noise of clanging pots was what woke up Mrs. Bashara.

"What's that smell?" she called out as soon as she and her husband were close to the kitchen, but neither of the girls seemed to hear.

"Oh, hi. Good morning, mum. Good morning, dad," Mira spewed as soon as she saw her parents.

"Good morning, honey. What's happening here?" Mrs. Bashara asked, glancing around the messy kitchen.

"Well, we woke up a little early, and decided to-" Mira began to explain.

"No. You woke up early, and then you wouldn't let me sleep," Liya butted in from a corner of the kitchen where she sat, watching the birds dance around outside from the window.

Anyway, I decided to try to make pancakes for everyone, and that's exactly what I'm doing," she gave a wide smile. "Just pancakes?" Mr. Bashara asked as he moved towards the kitchen.

There were sprinkles of flour all over the floor. It looked more like the twins were having a "flour-sprinkle fight" than that of anyone cooking.

"Yes. Just pancakes. I've made a few already. You should try one," Mira said, pointing to the tray of pancakes on the stove.

"Bad idea, mum," Liya said lazily from her seat.

"Shut up, Liya. Please try it, mum. You should taste it too, dad."

"Oh no, I haven't brushed my teeth. I'll come have a taste later," Mr. Bashara said, rushing towards the bathroom.

Mrs. Bashara was also about to excuse herself, but the look of hurt on Mira's face stopped her.

"Let's see what we have here," she said as she broke a piece off one of the pancakes with a fork and tasted it.

Mira looked up at her mum's face, observing her every reaction.

"So, what do you think, mum?"

Mrs. Bashara tried her best to hold back from coughing and put on an encouraging smile.

"Well, it's not that bad. It's just really greasy," she said as nicely as she could.

"Oh," Mira said, as her smile dimmed.

"Hey don't you be discouraged, at least you tried," Mrs. Bashara said, patting her on the shoulder.

"I warned you," Liya commented from her spot, but no one paid attention to her.

"Finish up with what you are doing and clean this place up. We're eating out this morning. There's this amazing breakfast diner a few meters away," Mrs. Bashara announced with a smile.

"But what about my pancakes?" Mira asked in a high-pitched voice.

"Oh, huh–let's place them in the fridge and we'll think about them later. How does that sound?"said Mrs. Bashara

"Good enough," Mira said as she turned off the gas stove.

"You should help your sister, Aliyah," Mrs. Bashara said.

"Okay," Liya grunted and got up without a fight.

Mrs. Bashara stepped out of the kitchen, all smiles. It was adorable that her girls thought of doing something tangible for the first time in a long time.

There was still a long way to go, but she loved the girls she just encountered in the kitchen. And despite that Liya hadn't been doing anything, Mrs. Bashara could see a spark of support in her eyes, and she knew that there was no sarcasm intended. She loved what she saw.

** ** ** ** **

Breakfast that morning was the warmest welcome the Bashara's has had in a long time. The older woman who owned the diner recognized Mr. Bashara and kept calling him by his first name. People the twins had never seen before came over to their table to greet them too and seemed happy to see them.

"Special treat for you and your family, Hakeem," the older lady said as she dropped an extra plate of pie before them. She was robust, and she had dimples that deepened when she smiled.

"Thank you, Rose," Mr. Bashara said with a wide smile. He had a look of gratitude and approval of Rose and the diner.

"These are your kids?" Rose asked, and Mr. Bashara nodded.

"Hey, girls. I'm glad to finally meet you. Aliyah and Amira, yes?" she asked.

"Yes, ma'am," the girls replied courteously.

"I'm Rose, and your father is like a son to me," she said, beaming, "So if you need anything else, just reach out, okay?"

"Yes, ma'am," they chorused.

"Thanks, Rose," Mrs. Bashara said, smiling widely.

"Oh come on, you know that I will do anything for you people just as you have always done for us," she said with a wave of a hand as she turned to leave for another table, retiring her apron along the way.

"Who is that?" Mira, who sat to her mum's right, asked.

"You heard her. She's Rose, and she owns the diner," Liya said.

"No, I meant, who is she to us?" Mira asked.

"She's just someone who thinks very highly of your father and his little philanthropic acts. When our cabin was still under construction, your father used to come here almost all the time to get to know the area and the locals better. However, everyone pretty much seems to mind their businesses here, as you can see," she said, signaling to the rest of the people in the room.

It was true, the girls noticed. The diner was superb, but it was a little empty. There was no unnecessary loud discussion from any table, and no one had come over to strike any meaningless conversation at their table either. They just said their "hello's" and moved along.

"The people here are very nice," Mr. Bashara joined in the conversation.

"Hmm. I think it's a little too bare, though. I mean, the food is nice. There should be more people," Liya commented before turning back to her plate.

"I think the weekdays account for the emptiness because most people come here for vacations. Notwithstanding, there's usually more influx during the weekends," Mr. Bashara explained.

"What are we going to do today, mum?" Mira asked, changing the topic suddenly.

"I'm thinking about spending time at the lake, play some games, fire up the grill much later, and maybe teach you some of my recipes if you're interested," Mrs. Bashara replied, stretching the last part slowly.

"I think that'd be great," Mira said matter-of-factly, "don't you agree, Liya?"

'Liya glared at her sister for a moment. She wasn't a fan of the heat that came with kitchens at all.

"I think I'll pass, thank you," she said with a fake smile, and her mum laughed.

"So, you'll just sit and do nothing while mum and I sweat in the kitchen?" Mira gave a false gasp.

"Oh well. That might be an exaggeration. You see, we wouldn't exactly be sweating per se," her mum chuckled, "we'd just be trying out some fundamental stuff–like pancakes, first of all."

"Awesome," Mira said, making loud noises with her fork.

"Maybe Aliya could help me out in the garage. I intend to do a little cleaning today. What do you say? Do we have a deal? Mr. Bashara asked. He was smiling too.

"Yes, it does," Mira said happily.

"Whatever," Liya commented, giving a slight chuckle.

The rest of that day was like a dream come true for the Basharas. They had a great time. It was precisely as Mrs. Bashara had envisioned. At some point, everyone checked their phones for messages and when it seemed like everyone was getting distracted by their phones, Mrs. Bashara seized them, and they had to win games before getting them back. Everyone, including her husband.

Much later that evening, when the girls went to the lake, they found some children lost and wandering. Even though the twins barely knew the vicinity themselves, they had helped get the children safely back to their parents. Mrs. Bashara was thrilled when she heard about the unselfish bravery of the twins. They had done so many things together as a family the past few days. Mrs. Bashara was feeling like she was in another world, so much so that when it was time to leave, none of them wanted to go. But work called.

"Mum, could we please stop by that town where we lodged the other night? We borrowed this book from a book store, and we need to return it," Liya said as soon as everyone was in the car, set to return home.

"Yeah, sure," Mrs. Bashara replied, putting on her seatbelt.

"All set?" their father called out. All set everyone replied, and off they went, away from the magical vacation wonderland.

In her heart, Liya wished that they could hang out like that more often, but she'd never admit it out loud. She looked at her hands and smiled as she remembered that her mum shoved scarves in their hands when they were leaving home. Surprisingly, she hadn't bothered them about it all through the weekend, except when it was time to pray.

The girls met Mr. Smith sitting in the same position as when he told them Franzel's story. There were two stools in front of him as though he had just entertained some children with a story.

"Haha. The twins," Mr. Smith said with a crinkled smile as soon as he saw them, "I've been expecting you."

"Yeah. We're sorry. It wasn't intentional. Here's your book," Liya said, placing the book on the counter with a loud thump. She was glad they were finally going to be rid of it.

"Thank you, girls." Mr. Smith said, still wearing his smile, "I hope the past few days have been exciting for you."

The girls exchanged glances before replying.

"Yes it has, thank you," Mira said.

"We have to leave now. Our parents are out waiting for us," she added.

"Very well, then. Hopefully, you'd drop by some other time. Send my regards to your parents," Mr. Smith said warmly.

"I'm never stepping in another book store again," Liya said under her breath, and her sister laughed. "We will," Mira said as she reached out to hold her sister's hand.

Together, they walked out the door with the little bell jingling behind them, and they made a silent, unwritten note to push the events of the past days behind them. A lot had changed, and they felt like different people, but they were going back to their familiar neighborhood, and although they will miss the cabin, it felt good to be going home.

CHAPTER SIX

The Stench of The Steel Mill

Laura fidgeted with the Bashara's house doorbell until Mira ran over to open the door and let her in.

"Hey, it's been a minute," Laura greeted excitedly with a wave and a big smile as she walked into the house.

"Hi, Laura. It's good to see you," Mira said, giving her a small hug.

"Ouu. You smell like spices," Laura commented, pulling away fast.

"Yeah, sorry," Mira said with a small laugh, "I'm working on this new recipe I found online, but it turned out to be a disaster."

"Recipe?" Laura laughed, expecting that it was some joke, but Mira nodded.

"That's new," Laura said cautiously with an awkward laugh.

"Is that Laura?" Liya yelled from somewhere inside the house.

"Yes, girlfriend. There can only be one with a voice so sweet," she eulogized herself, fanning her face with her fingers as she bounced onto the sofa.

Liya came running down the stairs quickly, and she jumped into Laura's arms. She really missed her friend.

"Heyy, it's so nice to see you again," Liya said breathlessly.

"It's good to see you too. I've been expecting you guys to drop by since forever. You didn't call either. I was starting to think something had gone wrong with you guys. What happened?" Laura asked as she pulled away from the embrace.

The twins exchanged looks, and Liya wondered how they would explain the very complicated events of the past days to their friend.

Their parents had also subtly instructed them against going to see the 'blonde-haired girl', and although it hadn't sounded like a strict warning, the girls hadn't been willing to take any chances by not heeding their parents' instructions.

"Come on, girls, fill me in on all of the fun. I'm inquisitive," Laura said in a high-pitched voice, "And while we are at it, could you please explain to me when Mira started to venture into cooking?"

"Well, mum's been teaching me some stuff, and I'm finding her tutorials quite interesting, so I've been practicing in my spare time," Mira said as she moved to sit opposite Laura.

"Wow. So you guys didn't go ahead with the plan?" Laura asked in surprise as she looked from Mira to Liya.

"Not even you, Liya?"

"We had a change of heart. And the trip turned out to be pretty interesting in the end," Liya explained with a shrug.

"Wow," Laura remarked quietly, "Anyway, since you girls have no juicy talk for me, I am going to present you with mine. You know I never disappoint."

"What's up?" Liya asked eagerly.

"Remember the party I told you I was planning before you left?"

"Yes?"

"Well it's this weekend. I mean, Sunday evening, and we are so going to attend because I managed to get myself two extra passes. Can I get a scream?" Laura screeched.

The girls were elated at the news, and Mira broke into a happy dance as Liya screamed.

"Everyone from school is going to be there. At least every important person. And believe me, it's going to be a bomb. No one would be able to stop talking about it till school resumes. I wish I could show you the plans that we, the organizing committee, have in store for you guys, but it's best left as a surprise, so I can't. I'm sorry, girls," Laura bragged.

The girls laughed and let their imaginations go for a ride.

"I can't wait. Do you think we should have a dress code?" Mira asked.

"Of course. And you know what else I think we should have? A car. An exclusive luxury car. It will be the best appearance of the night, believe me," Laura said.

"Huh–okay," Mira replied, hesitantly, "but how are we going to get a car?"

"We could be dropped off by our parents' of course. However, at the moment, my parents are away on separate business trips and won't be home on Sunday. So that leaves us with one option. We have to go with your parents'," She said flatly.

"I don't think that'll be a good idea," Mira retorted immediately.

"Why not? There are four cars in your garage."

"Well, for one, none of us here can drive," Liya pointed out matter-of-factly.

"And even if we could, we're not old enough to get licenses," Mira added.

"Exactly," Liya said.

Laura chuckled, "Relax, girls. I've thought about all these roadblocks, so chill.

My silly brother owes me a favor, so I'm going to ask him to be our chaperone/chauffeur. That settles it."

"Does your brother have a license?" Mira asked.

"No. But he can drive. He drives my mum to get stuff around the neighborhood sometimes," Laura said with a shrug.

"Yeah. Because that's about the farthest he can go without a license," Mira pointed out.

"Whatever," Laura said, "So are you guys in?"

"I don't know. We have to ask our parents first," Liya said, and her sister gave the nod in agreement.

"You have got to be kidding me," Laura said, laughing.

"What's funny?" Mira asked with a straight face.

"What's not funny? When did the Bashara twins ever have to ask their mummy and daddy for permission?"

The twins rolled their eyes and paid no attention to Laura's taunting words.

"What has come over you two?" Laura asked again.

When Mira and Liya still didn't reply, she rose to her feet to leave.

"Fine. Go suck up to your parents or whatever. I'll come by tomorrow to hear how that turns out. But from experience, believe me when I say that it won't turn out well," she said conclusively before she let herself out of the house.

True to Laura's words, Mr. and Mrs. Bashara were against the idea. At first, they opted to drive the girls themselves but realized that they had a corporate dinner to attend at Mrs. Bashara's office that same night. But at least they permitted the girls to attend the party, giving them a curfew, of course.

When Laura came by the following day, she teased them mercilessly. Reminding them about the previous conversations they used to have, talks about how parents were out only to suck the fun out of their children's lives.

"Curfews? Permissions? Rules? That's not our thing, remember? And parents will keep preying on you until you prove that to them. So, ladies, what's it going to be? Are we going to be cowardly chickens or the dauntless girls we've always been?" Laura encouraged them.

Slowly, she broke the girls' resolve, and when Sunday evening came, they all set out from the Bashara's house dressed fashionably, with Laura's brother as their chauffeur. If at any time the twins remembered Franzel or Mr. Smith's story, they didn't show it. The cursed book was no longer in their possession after all. They were out to have the night of their lives. And they did. As Laura had predicted, their entrance was mind-blowing with their father's exquisite car, and the party was boisterous. But what the girls didn't know early enough was that the party wasn't going to be the only thing about that night that they would forever have etched in their young memories.

✳✳ ✳✳ ✳✳ ✳✳ ✳✳ ✳✳

Fatigued from all the fun at the party, the girls slumped in the car–the twins in the back seat, Laura on the passenger's seat in front, and her brother before the steering.

"Oh, crap. We're almost past our curfew," Mira said, peering at her wristwatch with the aid of the streetlights. "Let's go," Laura said, nudging her brother.

There was some presence of alcohol at the party, and although the girls had promised themselves to steer clear of it, Laura looked a little tipsy.

Her brother started the engine and was about to move the car when he paused.

"Do you guys smell that?" He asked, turning to face the twins, but it appeared that they didn't hear him.

"What?" Laura asked drowsily, "just drive, silly."

"Right," he said as he returned his eyes to the road.

After driving a few meters away from the noise and bustle, he stopped abruptly, startling all the occupants of the car. The road was quiet.

"What was that for?" Laura asked crossly.

"I'm sorry, but how are you guys not smelling this stink in this car?" He asked as he pulled over to one side of the road and opened the door to let fresh air in.

"Are you drunk?" Laura yelled, sitting up properly in her seat.

"No, he's not. I smell it too," Liya said quietly as her eyes widened in horror. The reek was familiar, and it could not be mistaken.

"I smell it too," Mira whispered. She was starting to hear her heart thump loudly in her chest.

"Oh, crude. I just caught the whiff now, too," Laura said finally, "let's get out of here, brother. This neighborhood is a foul-smelling one."

"It's not the neighborhood," Liya whispered, but Laura couldn't hear from her seat.

The one-legged slave was real–the girls realized. They also knew that the only way to get the stench to go was to retrace their steps by getting to their parents and apologizing as soon as possible. And that meant they needed to get home fast.

"Laura is right. We should get going," Mira said, starting to panic.

"I can't drive like this. The stench is too strong," Laura's brother protested.

"All the more reason why we should leave on time, dumbhead," Laura bellowed.

"Okay, okay," He finally agreed, and he came back into the car and fastened his seat belt first before closing the door. Just as he started the engine yet again and the lights came on, he inhaled sharply.

"What is it again?" Laura protested.

"I-I saw someone in front of the car," he said. He looked horrified.

"He just flashed for a second and went away, like smoke."

"You, my brother, are drunk," Laura said, patting his shoulder in mock concern.

The older boy shrugged, but his hands were shaking now. Managing to put himself together, he drove on, but just as he was about to round the bend, he lost control of the wheel and crashed into a pole with a loud screech.

The twins gasped in alarm as they all dashed out of the car to see the damage. First off, Franzel's stench still hung in the air, and on top of that, they had just bashed their father's car. They thought it couldn't get any worse.

"Look!" Laura's brother exclaimed, pointing in a direction. Right there before them was the shadowy figure of a man. He was there long enough for the twins to take in his appearance. He wore an old-fashioned coat with its buttons hanging on a thread and held an axe in hand. His hair stood high above his head like broomsticks, and he had dark holes for eyes. But what frightened them the most was his bottom half; protruding out of his shorts was just one leg. Where the other leg should have been, there was nothing–nothing but the darkness of the night as the wind toyed with the fabric of the shorts.

As if on cue, they all screamed together until he disappeared again.

"What the hell was THAT?" Laura's brother asked panting.

"Franzel," Mira answered.

"You know that man? I mean, the ghost or whatever that was?" Laura asked breathlessly. She didn't look even the slightest bit tipsy anymore.

"Yes, and he's here to punish us for not listening to our pa–"Liya began to explain, but she stopped,

"What?" Laura asked, looking up at Liya's face, which looked frozen in terror. She seemed to be looking at something behind Laura.

"He's behind you, Laura. Run!" Her brother yelled, and all four of them scampered. The road was straight, leaving them with only one direction to run towards. They kept screaming as they dashed away, but it didn't matter how fast they ran; Franzel seemed to be floating towards them fast.

"Help!" Laura screamed as she tripped and sprained an ankle. Her brother was way in front, but on seeing his sister. He turned back to help her.

"No, no, please don't go back. Franzel is close. He will chop off your legs, please," Liya said with teary eyes as soon as she saw what he was about to do.

"I can't leave my sister," he bellowed in response and continued running.

"Come on, Liya, we need to keep going," Mira said frantically, tugging at her sister's hand, but Liya wouldn't move. She just stared back at Laura and her brother, he was trying to lift her onto his back. She saw Franzel float closer to them, and she looked on in fear.

"Please, Liya. We need to go," Mira cried, and this time Liya agreed. As they ran on, they heard a loud, piercing scream from

Laura's brother, and they felt their hearts melt in dread. The cry could only mean one thing; the ghost had caught up with their friends.

The girls didn't stop running. Their fear pumped harder, fueling them as they ran in the direction of their house.

Soon enough, they could see their house, and they felt joy flood through their bodies as they reduced their paces into jogs, but Franzel had other plans for them.

"Nasty, vile, stubborn-,"they heard a coarse thundering voice say from behind them.

The girls screamed again and ran faster, but as they rounded the last bend to their block, they found Franzel standing right in the middle of the road, waiting for them.

"You were warned but you wouldn't listen," he thundered as he walked towards them. With each step he took, the ground seemed to shake, and the girls were immobilized by fright. The one-legged man reached out both of his huge hands and swatted at the girls to catch them as though they were flies, but he missed. Mira felt a cold chill seep into her body as he touched them, and she felt her senses return. They couldn't just stand there and let the ghost get them. They had to do something. So she did the first thing she could think of.

As Franzel swatted at them the second time, she grabbed hold of her sister's hand, and they ducked and ran as fast as they could. If only they could just get home, they knew all would be well.

Soon enough, they made it to their porch, and as Liya struggled to get the key into the hole despite her shaky hands, Franzel inched closer, laughing loudly.

Just as he was about to get within arm's length, the door opened, and they busted in, bolting it tightly after them.

"Aliyah, Amirah. We've been waiting up for you," Mrs. Bashara said as she walked towards them in her night robe. The girls rushed into her arms and began to cry. Confused, Mrs. Bashara patted their hair gently.

"We're so sorry, mom," Liya cried, sniffing deeply. The stench was gone, she noticed. But then she saw something else. In between her sister's black hair, some strands had gone gray, and she knew that it would be the same for hers too. She thought about Laura and where she must be, or what might have happened to her and her brother, but it only made her break down in more tears.

That night, Mrs. Bashara accompanied the girls to their rooms as she used to do when they were younger, and as she kissed their foreheads, she asked that they save their explanations for the next day.

The girls had trouble sleeping that night. Franzel had left them an important lesson, and they knew that they would never again attempt to go against their parents. Ever. Franzel was gone, but they knew he would always be lurking, watching closely for any small act of rebellion.

www.ingramcontent.com/pod-product-compliance
Lightning Source LLC
Chambersburg PA
CBHW031546310726
48971CB00008B/2650